HOW SELF-DRIVING CARS WILL IMPACT SOCIETY

by Jessica Mosloski

ReferencePoint Press®

San Diego, CA

TECHNOLOGY'S IMPACT

For more information, contact:
ReferencePoint Press, Inc.
PO Box 27779
San Diego, CA 92198
www.ReferencePointPress.com

LIBRARY OF CONGRESS CATALOGING-IN-PUBLICATION DATA

Name: Mosloski, Jessica, 1994– author.
Title: How Self-Driving Cars Will Impact Society / by Jessica Mosloski.
Description: San Diego, CA : ReferencePoint Press, Inc., [2018] | Series: Technology's Impact | Includes bibliographical references and index. | Audience: Grades 9 to 12.
Identifiers: LCCN 2018011546 (print) | LCCN 2018013172 (ebook) | ISBN 9781682824986 (ebook) | ISBN 9781682824979 (hardback)
Subjects: LCSH: Autonomous vehicles—Juvenile literature. | Automobile transportation—Technological innovations—Social aspects—Juvenile literature.
Classification: LCC TL152.8 (ebook) | LCC TL152.8 .M67 2018 (print) | DDC 629.2—dc23
LC record available at https://lccn.loc.gov/2018011546

Contents

IMPORTANT EVENTS IN THE DEVELOPMENT OF **SELF-DRIVING CARS**

1921
An early version of a driverless car is demonstrated in Ohio. It is controlled by cables from another car following it.

1925
Engineers in New York City introduce a radio-controlled car called the "Linrrican Wonder."

1950s–1960s
Driverless cars are developed that can be controlled by circuits under the roadways.

1980s
Development of more advanced driverless car technology begins in Japan, Europe, and the US.

1920 | 1935 | 1950 | 1975 | 1990

1939
In its Futurama exhibit at the New York World's Fair, General Motors presents a vision of the future that features vehicles driving themselves down superhighways.

1991
The US Congress passes the Intermodal Surface Transportation Efficiency Act. It includes a directive to the US Department of Transportation to develop a prototype of a highway system for automated vehicles.

2004 2008 2012 2016 2020

2004
The first Defense Advanced Research Projects Agency (DARPA) race for self-driving cars takes place in a desert, but none of the vehicles finish.

2005
The second DARPA race is held. This time, five of the self-driving cars finish.

2007
The third DARPA race takes place in an urban setting, proving that driverless cars can function in cities.

2012
Google introduces its first self-driving car to the world.

2015
Tesla Motors releases its Autopilot technology, enabling limited self-driving capabilities in some of its cars.

2016
At least thirty large automakers and technology firms are developing driverless car technology.

2017
Cruise Automation, owned by General Motors, works with the state of New York to prepare to launch a self-driving car program there in 2018.

2017
The US House of Representatives unanimously approves a bill that encourages the development of self-driving cars.

2018
The California Department of Motor Vehicles plans to begin issuing permits for testing driverless cars on public roads.

Self-Driving Cars Today

Imagine looking across the street to your neighbor's house one morning and seeing his new, shiny car back smoothly out of the garage. You have seen this happen hundreds of times as he is about to leave for work each morning. But something is different about this new car now idling in the driveway—the driver is nowhere in sight! Minutes later, your neighbor exits the house and climbs into the car waiting for him just outside his front door. Your eyes do not deceive you. The company Tesla has built a car that can be summoned from a short distance using only a smartphone app. This feature saves a driver the inconvenience of having to climb in and out of the car when it is parked in a tight space. Automated features like this are small but significant steps along the path to deploying self-driving cars onto our roadways.

THE DEFINITION OF SELF-DRIVING CARS

Self-driving cars, which can also be referred to as driverless vehicles or **autonomous** and connected vehicles (AV/CV), have been defined by University of California researchers Adam Stocker and Susan Shaheen as "vehicles used to move passengers or freight with some level of automation that aims to assist or replace human control."[1] This technology has the potential to drastically change the automobile industry. It could also change roads, cities, and the activities of people. Self-driving car researcher Michael König wrote,

"The automotive industry is currently undergoing a potentially revolutionary change that could not only affect how vehicles are built but also reshape the design of roads and cities as well as the interaction between humans and machines."[2]

WORDS IN CONTEXT

autonomous
Acting independently or having the freedom to do so.

THE TECHNOLOGY IN SELF-DRIVING CARS

Automobile technology has now developed to a point where self-driving cars are being tested on public roadways by several different automakers. According to Mark Fields, CEO of Ford Motors, Ford is planning to release a vehicle by 2021 that has "no gas pedal, no steering wheel, and the passenger will never need to take control of the vehicle in a predefined area."[3] The gas pedal and steering wheel, considered standard in non-autonomous vehicles, are being replaced by technology including cameras, GPS, radar, LIDAR, and other sensors to detect, interpret, and react to the environment around the vehicle. "Together, this system provides a view of the world that a driver alone cannot access, seeing in every direction simultaneously, and on wavelengths that go far beyond the human senses," Tesla said on its website.[4]

The vehicles hosting this technology are being developed with different levels of automation, each of which gives the human driver varying degrees of control over driving. Because of these different degrees of automation, it is sometimes not clear which functions will belong to the role of the driver versus the role of the car. Engineering researcher Miltos Kyriakidis notes that, although self-driving cars have

Cars with higher levels of automation are still in testing stages. Several companies are working to explore this technology.

great potential to improve the lives of motorists, "The role of human drivers within the automated vehicle is not yet clearly established."[5] However, what is clear is that, in the years to come, self-driving cars will influence many aspects of society. Mobility planning expert Shannon McDonald has said of self-driving cars, "This will completely change us as a society. I think it'll have the same transformational change as the introduction of the automobile."[6]

SELF-DRIVING CARS AND SOCIETY

As self-driving cars are integrated into society, many experts predict they will follow a pattern similar to the introduction of automobiles years ago. Cars have had a huge cultural impact. Cities, industries, and lifestyles have been reshaped by the invention of automobiles. Cars represented the ideals of efficiency and industry that shaped our nation in the twentieth century. But automobiles were originally met with hostility by many when they were introduced on American roads. It took time for automobiles to become the necessity that they are today. As self-driving cars have developed, they've already seen some pushback. However, many companies are still pursuing this technology. They believe self-driving cars will add convenience to everyday life.

Research has shown that this technology has many advantages, such as improving convenience, efficiency, safety, and eco-friendliness. However, self-driving cars also come with a myriad of challenges, including winning over wary consumers, eliminating traditional jobs held by human drivers, and causing cities to have to reevaluate their infrastructure. The technology also brings up questions about privacy, hacking, liability, and legislation. Although there will be hurdles to overcome, self-driving cars appear to have a bright future and the potential to change our society for the better.

Chapter 1

What Is the Technology Behind Self-Driving Cars?

Several key pieces of technology make self-driving cars possible. This includes various sensors and cameras. They work together to create the eyes and ears of the car, replacing the senses of a human driver. With this technology, cars have been categorized into five levels of **automation**. The highest level of automation describes cars that are fully self-driving.

NAVIGATION TECHNOLOGY

The global positioning system (GPS) is an indispensable part of a self-driving car. It was developed for military applications during the 1980s and became available for commercial use in 1995. It has been widely used in the automotive industry ever since. This technology is already familiar to most people with smartphones, and many cars today already come equipped with GPS mapping capabilities. GPS works by interpreting signals returning from a network of satellites orbiting Earth. The GPS signals travel at the speed of light from the satellites to a GPS device, such as a smartphone, on Earth. The time it takes for these signals to travel is used to calculate the GPS device's location.

In addition to letting people know their exact location in the world at any time, GPS also plays a part in helping drivers navigate and avoid traffic. This technology, combined with information picked up by cameras and other sensors, could also help self-driving cars plot their own detailed maps as they drive through new locations. GPS is accurate within a few yards when tracking anything, including the location of a self-driving car. Camera and sensor technologies in self-driving cars provide more detailed information that pinpoints exactly where the vehicle is on the road. When using a self-driving car to make a map, these cameras and sensors could help flesh out the maps with details like signs, buildings, and stoplights.

> **WORDS IN CONTEXT**
>
> **automation**
>
> A system or technique that reduces human input, instead using computer technology to operate on its own.

Self-driving cars rely heavily on cameras, and there are multiple cameras in each car. One function of these cameras is to keep the vehicle in its lane. As the car drives, it takes photos of the lane markings on the roads. Those photos are then processed by a computer, which uses that information to let other parts of the car know if they need to adjust the car's direction. Additionally, the cameras let the car know what else is happening behind and in front of the car. Backup cameras have already become a common driver-assistance feature in many cars, and they are vital to the operation of self-driving vehicles.

Self-driving cars also navigate by using radar, which stands for radio detection and ranging. Radar works by sending out radio waves that hit objects in the vicinity and then bounce back to be analyzed by computers. The amount of time it takes the wave to return helps the computers detect how close other vehicles or obstacles are and how fast they are moving. This helps the self-driving car make sure that it doesn't crash into anything.

Self-driving cars are equipped with many sensors, cameras, and other technologies. The cars use these to navigate the world around them.

Self-driving cars also use LIDAR, which is similar to radar. LIDAR sends out rapid pulses of invisible light—more than 1 million per second—that bounce off nearby objects. The returning light is then detected by sensors on the vehicle. This data is used to create 3D images of the surrounding environment. It is also used to measure the speed of other vehicles. The LIDAR system sits on the roof of the car so that it can capture a 360-degree rotating view of its surroundings. Some LIDAR systems are accurate down to just 0.8 inches (2 cm). Although LIDAR is an integral component of self-driving cars, the technology is not cheap. The roof-mounted laser system used by Google, an Internet technology company that is investing heavily in self-driving cars, has been reported to cost around $80,000.

Infrared sensors are another important component of self-driving cars. Like LIDAR, infrared sensors send out waves of light that are invisible to the human eye. This helps the car detect people and animals that may be hard to see at night with just the cameras. They also pick up living things better than radar, which is more suited for detecting solid, metallic objects, such as other vehicles.

Ultrasonic sensors provide cars with even more data about the world around them. They work by picking up sound waves that cannot be heard by human ears. In self-driving cars, ultrasonic sensors are used to detect nearby objects such as sidewalks and curbs. Similar to radar, ultrasonic waves bounce back to the sender, which then analyzes them to determine if there is enough space to back up, park, or make other movements.

The data picked up by this plethora of sensors is analyzed and interpreted by a computer that acts as the brain of the vehicle. As science and engineering researcher Gautam Shroff explains, "[The software] 'brain' must connect all the inputs it receives so as to predict the immediate future, including the likely paths that nearby moving cars might take. Finally, all these predictions must be processed and converted into directions to the car's steering wheel, accelerator, and brake to continually correct the car's trajectory."[7] Because the computer must make the vehicle react in real time, it makes hundreds of thousands of calculations in a single second.

COMMUNICATION TECHNOLOGY

In addition to the technology helping each self-driving car operate independently, technology is being developed to allow these vehicles to talk to one another. Currently, cars are all isolated from each other on the road. There is no technology enabling them to communicate directly. The main ways drivers are able to communicate with each other are using their turn signals, flashing their lights, or honking their horns. But these communications are imprecise and can lead to miscommunication or even dangerous misunderstandings. With vehicle-to-vehicle (V2V) technology, which is defined by the National Highway Traffic Safety Administration (NHTSA) as the "dynamic wireless exchange of data between nearby vehicles,"[8] cars would be able to warn each other of dangerous conditions. "Once deployed, V2V will provide 360-degree situational awareness on the road and will help us enhance vehicle safety," said former US Transportation Secretary Anthony Foxx.[9] V2V technology is considered essential for self-driving cars. For example, a car on the freeway could warn cars behind it about a patch of ice or a piece of debris on the road. Then those cars could begin taking action to steer clear of the hazard. V2V technology could even potentially eliminate the need for traffic signals in the future as self-driving cars decide on their own which ones have the right of way at certain points in time. Whether the car is completely automated or has some features that are still controlled by a human driver, V2V technology could play a huge part in safety and coordination on the road.

SMART ROADS VS. SMART CARS

Several of the early models of self-driving cars developed in the 1950s and 1960s were based on the idea of smart roads. Rather than making cars filled with the devices and systems that allow for self-driving, the concept of smart roads envisioned mechanisms of control embedded in a road itself. "In some implementation, automated highways are inevitable," Bob Ervin of the University of Michigan's Transportation Research Institute, said in 1988.[10] Such systems do operate today, but they are limited to vehicles that follow a fixed path, such as trains. The automobile industry's focus has since shifted to developing technology within the cars themselves.

Self-driving cars have many sensors that allow them to assess their surroundings. Companies are also developing cars that will be able to communicate with each other through technology.

This technology has proven to be much more successful for a few reasons. First, going the route of smart roads would require astronomically expensive updates to existing roads. Secondly, most vehicles would need to be outfitted with updated communication technology to operate on smart roads. Finally, the technology in cars has gradually become more and more automated since they were first introduced. Self-driving automation is the logical next step. Many advanced features, such as GPS systems and back-up cameras, are already in many cars today. These features have continued to develop over the years. As cameras and computers have become smaller and more efficient over the decades, putting them in an autonomous car has become more feasible.

LEVELS OF AUTOMATION

A fully automated self-driving car could have a vast array of applications and features. Imagine a sleek, futuristic vehicle driving up and opening the door on its own. Perhaps the inside includes a TV screen on the ceiling, windows that display information about places it drives by, and lighting that can self-adjust to fit a rider's mood. As an added touch, the self-driving car could respond to a host of voice commands, from changing its driving route to making a cup of coffee for a passenger. Although this all seems like a far-away fantasy, self-driving cars already exist and are even on the road right now. However, it is important to remember that cars can be automated to different levels. They do not necessarily need to have all these flashy features to be automated. In order to distinguish among various levels of automation, the NHTSA has defined six levels of self-driving vehicles. They range from the driver having complete manual control of the vehicle—Level Zero—to the car having completely automated control of itself—Level Five.

AUTOMATION THROUGH THE YEARS

When cars were first invented in the early 1900s, there was very little automation in their functions. Lights had to be manually turned on, and doors and windows had to be opened manually. These vehicles were what the NHTSA would now define as Level Zero, or nonautonomous. The human driver controlled all aspects of driving, from starting and acceleration to steering and braking, at all times, with no assistance by any automatic systems. As more and more people began to drive cars, automakers began to see the limitations of the technology. Over time, manufacturers began to improve the automobile by adding what are now standard features such as turn signals, brake lights, safety glass, and headlamps.

The addition of GPS systems in cars is one feature that helped vehicle automation technology advance from Level One to Level Two. Cruise control and automatic transmission are other features that furthered vehicle automation.

By the end of the 1900s, cars progressed from Level Zero, which is complete manual control, to Level One, which is function-specific automation. In other words, there are a few automated features for specific functions, such as pre-charged brakes, electronic stability control, and automated, rather than crank, windows. However, a human driver is still needed for most functions. Over the years, additional features were added such as power steering (1951), cruise control (1958), and navigation systems (1995). Society smoothly progressed from using Level Zero vehicles to using Level One vehicles because the technological advancements were gradually added, allowing drivers plenty of time to learn and adapt to the innovations.

Between the mid-1990s and the 2000s, automotive technology advanced to the point where self-driving cars were becoming a real possibility. GPS systems had become more accurate and were able to download updated maps automatically. Adaptive cruise control (ACC), a feature necessary for self-driving cars, was developed in the 1990s. ACC is a system that uses radar or a **stereo camera** in the vehicle to tell the car to brake when it detects the car is approaching another vehicle ahead, then accelerate when traffic allows. This is different from standard cruise control, which allows the driver to set a desired speed but does not automatically adjust the speed if it senses a slower-moving car ahead. The invention of ACC and dual clutch transmission, which allows cars to change gears automatically at faster rates, helped the automation of cars bridge the gap between Level One and Level Two. Level Two is the first level at which portions of the car could be considered "self-driving."

WORDS IN CONTEXT

stereo camera

A camera system that uses at least two separate lenses and image sensors to simulate the binocular vision of humans and produce three-dimensional pictures.

Level Two cars use combined function automation, meaning certain aspects of the vehicle are automated to the point that they can work together to control their part of the driving task while the human driver continues the role of observing and controlling the remaining driving responsibilities. Other Level Two features include systems to detect blind spots, center the vehicle in its lane, and self-park. Multiple functions combine to make these features possible. For example, with blind spot detector technology, sensors on the sides of vehicles alert the driver if another car is in its blind spot when merging.

Cameras mounted on the windshield help cars with lane-centering technology detect lane markings. With parking assistance systems, the driver controls the gas pedal while an onboard computer takes over steering when parallel parking.

By 2017, Level Two automation was the highest level available for consumers. It is mostly found in certain luxury car models. Volvo, Mercedes-Benz, and Infiniti offer vehicles with radar-based cruise control that can control and adjust the speed of the car even in heavy traffic. They also have systems that automatically steer to keep the car in its lane or slam on the brakes in an emergency situation. Volkswagen uses **thermal** technology to sense objects such as other cars, animals, and trees, then project images of them onto the windshield. Others offer night vision technology, which uses infrared sensors in the headlights to detect obstacles that cannot easily be seen in the dark. Ford and Mercedes-Benz offer this feature in some models. For the most part, Level Two automation technologies act as warning and crash-avoidance systems. The thermal and night vision technologies, which mostly focus on the detection of objects around the vehicle, are essential to overall Level Two automation because they are the first step in the detection and reaction process. With Level One automation, that process is completely handled by the human driver. In Level Two, after the systems collect information with sensors, they communicate with the driver or, in some cases, directly with the steering and braking systems of the car to take the necessary action.

WORDS IN CONTEXT

thermal
Relating to heat.

The next step in automation, Level Three, is known as limited self-driving automation. With Level Three, the vehicle can take over

5 LEVELS OF VEHICLE AUTOMATION

	What is it?	What features does it have?	Is it on the road now?
Level 0	No automation	No self-driving features	Yes
Level 1	Automation for specific functions	Cruise control	Yes
Level 2	Combined function automation, meaning some automated features work together to provide a higher level of automation	Center the vehicle in its lane, self-park	Yes, it's the highest level available to consumers
Level 3	Limited self-driving automation, meaning the car can drive on its own, but the human driver must be ready to take control when alerted by the car	Self-driving	No, but some companies are testing
Level 4	Fully self-driving under certain conditions	Self-driving	No, but some companies are testing
Level 5	Fully self-driving	Self-driving	No

control of parts of the driving and monitoring responsibilities, but the human driver must be ready to resume control when alerted by the automated system. Level Four takes the automation a step further, allowing the vehicle to control all the monitoring and driving functions without a human driver but only under certain environmental conditions. Level Five is the highest level of vehicle automation, where the vehicle can control all the monitoring and driving functions in place of a human driver under any environmental conditions.

The three highest levels of automation require a shift in the relationship between vehicle and human driver. Drivers must be confident that they can give control of the car over to the automated system. For that to happen, the automation technology must be proven to be safe and reliable. By early 2018, that shift hadn't happened yet. So, for now, it wouldn't be safe for those high-level self-driving cars to hit the road. But, there are several automakers working to make Level Three and Level Four automatic vehicles available to the public. About a dozen companies have claimed their cars will be equipped with at least Level Four automation by 2020. As of late 2017, "no automaker has set a timeline for bringing a Level Five car to market," according to automotive technology writer Jake Lingeman.[11] A 2014 study by research firm IHS Automotive suggests that complete automation—Level Five—could be available by 2030.

Although automakers are optimistic, some researchers offer words of caution. They believe that complete automation may never be possible, particularly in urban areas or other busy driving environments. Some experts say it would be better to focus on a system that works with and supports human drivers rather than one that completely replaces them. The most practical applications of this would be using automation in specific areas, such as highway driving.

THE DARPA RACES

Some of the most important events leading to the widespread development of self-driving cars were the DARPA Grand Challenges, a series of three races for self-driving cars held between 2004 and 2007. DARPA, the Defense Advanced Research Projects Agency, is part of the US Department of Defense. The agency specializes in developing military technologies, among other research projects.

In the early 2000s, DARPA Director Tony Tether was looking for a new project to bring positive attention to the agency. With his guidance, agency directors created a robotic car race dubbed the DARPA Grand Challenge. The course covered 142 miles (229 km) of treacherous desert terrain from California to Nevada. The winner of the race would earn $1 million. This race did not have any direct connections to the military or weapons development, which are the agency's primary focuses, and there were some initial fears that the project would end up backfiring.

However, the public's reaction to the race on March 13, 2004, surpassed all expectations. Thousands of people and national media outlets came to watch the race. There were fifteen contestants, mostly teams from universities or transportation corporations, in the final round of the competition. The competing vehicles were familiar models—including a Toyota, a Honda, and a Chevrolet—that were outfitted with bulky cameras, sensors, and other equipment. *Wired* magazine calls them a "motley assortment of driverless Frankencars."[12] Science and technology reporter Sharon Weinberger explains: "The individual technologies needed to build self-driving cars were all available, in theory, but pulling them together seemed like a nearly impossible feat, or at least something that had simply never been done before. It would be a mental advance, as much as a technical one, and Tether hoped the contest would spark nationwide interest in robotics."[13] Despite the media hype, none of the fifteen competing vehicles made it more than 8 miles (13 km). Some dropped out, experienced software malfunctions, became stuck, or crashed through fences. The last remaining vehicle ended up with its "belly straddling the outer edge of a drop-off, front wheels spinning freely, on fire,"[14] according to *Popular Science* magazine. Not one competitor could claim the $1 million prize, and *Popular Science* dubbed the race the "Debacle in the Desert."[15]

GOOGLE'S SELF-DRIVING CAR

Google made an announcement about developing self-driving cars in a blog post in October 2010. At the time, what set Google's self-driving cars apart from other models was that, while many others did not progress much past crude prototypes being tested in parking lots, Google's vehicles had already driven themselves hundreds of thousands of miles on busy roads, including crossing the Golden Gate Bridge, traversing Hollywood Boulevard, and navigating rush-hour traffic. They were able to navigate the complex road conditions by gathering, processing, and reacting to information in real time. In just a few more years, Google's self-driving cars traveled nearly 1 million miles (1.6 million km) with only one serious accident. However, Google points out that the accident occurred during a period that a human driver was in control. "Google believes that its AI self-driving system will consistently make the smartest, safest decision for the occupants of the vehicle as well as pedestrians or other users sharing the road; safer than even a human driver," according to *Fortune* magazine. Google pioneered the way to legally testing self-driving cars on public roadways after petitioning federal regulators to view self-driving systems as the "driver" in the car.

Quoted in Kirsten Korosec, "The Artificial Intelligence in Google's Self-Driving Cars Now Qualifies as Legal Driver," *Fortune*, February 2016. www.fortune.com.

Google is one of several technology companies that has heavily invested in self-driving cars. The technology has greatly improved over the past decade.

The first DARPA Grand Challenge highlighted some of the limitations of driverless vehicle technology. However, it also opened the door to making further improvements where earlier robotic vehicles fell short. The second Grand Challenge was set for 2005, and excitement still surrounded the competition despite the challenges of the previous race. Several of the same competitors entered. Carnegie Mellon University, Stanford University, and many others put their vehicles on the course that was even more dangerous than the first DARPA race course. It had cliffs, sharp turns, and rocky terrain. Although the vehicles were slow moving, with the winner averaging about 19 miles per hour (31 km/h), five vehicles ended up crossing the finish line. Stanford University took first place and claimed the

$2 million prize. According to Weinberger, "The Grand Challenge did not produce any new technology; its success was simply in demonstrating that self-driving cars would work."[16]

The third Grand Challenge competition was held in 2007 in California. It was named the Urban Challenge as it took place on a city-like course that required the competitors to obey traffic laws and avoid crashes. Out of the eleven teams that entered the final round, six finished, with Carnegie Mellon winning the challenge. The race was featured on magazines and in TV documentaries. The race proved that a future with self-driving cars, though still requiring significant developments, was possible.

Spurred on by his win of the 2005 DARPA challenge, Stanford computer science professor Sebastian Thrun took his expertise to Google and helped the company develop its driverless car, which it presented in 2012. DARPA's Grand Challenge competitions achieved their goal of proving that self-driving car technology was within reach. The races helped bridge the gap between the idea of self-driving cars and the reality.

Chapter 2

What Is the Positive Impact of Self-Driving Cars on Society?

Because cars play such a large part in society and everyday life, self-driving cars have the potential to greatly improve the lives of people who use them. Forty-five percent of people's daily car trips are used for shopping and errands, and 27 percent are used for social and recreational activities such as visiting friends or family. The remaining trips are used for commuting to and from work. With all of these trips, Americans end up traveling a combined 11 billion miles (18 billion km) each day. That's nearly 40 miles (64 km) daily per person.

"The amount of time the average driver spends behind the wheel each year is equivalent to seven 40-hour weeks at the office," says Jurek Grabowski, research director for the AAA Foundation for Traffic Safety.[17] Currently, vehicles function primarily as machines used to carry a person from point A to point B. One benefit of replacing traditional vehicles with self-driving cars is that the car is transformed from merely a transportation machine to a productive workspace or a relaxing space. Traveling time would turn into extended work or sleep hours. Even if nothing productive was being accomplished, the ride might be more enjoyable. Self-driving cars would free up mental space to allow people to eat, talk, read, or admire the surrounding scenery without needing to constantly pay attention to the road.

CARS AND INFRASTRUCTURE

Cars do not only have direct influence over how people travel. They also influence where people work, what they eat, where they shop, and with whom they socialize. Before automobiles were common in American society, people tended to work, shop, and socialize in the communities where they lived. Cars allowed people to move their lives to the suburbs, where land was less expensive, because they had highways to connect them to places they needed to go. The shift to automobile use affected the way cities were built as well. New types of businesses, including drive-throughs and convenience stores, began popping up, and parking structures and wider roads were built to accommodate the changes. When self-driving cars become widespread, they are likely to have a similarly transformative impact on infrastructure.

Some experts believe the use of self-driving cars will encourage people to move back to cities. They say that lowering the number of cars on city roads and reducing **congestion** will make parking and traveling in the city easier. According to engineering researcher Hubert Iglinski, "A frequently observed lack of traffic fluidity is, to a great extent, the drivers' fault and this affects the level of congestion. Therefore, AV [automatic vehicles] should be extremely beneficial in urbanized areas as those are the parts particularly exposed to traffic congestion."[18] However, others insist that self-driving cars will

> **WORDS IN CONTEXT**
>
> **congestion**
> Crowded or blocked, such as in traffic.

Self-driving cars are expected to transform many aspects of the way people use automobiles every day. For example, some experts believe self-driving cars could reduce traffic congestion.

make suburban life more appealing as people might not mind long commutes when they are able to read, rest, or work while they are traveling. Either way, driverless cars open up many more possibilities to the people who use them.

Anticipating the value that self-driving cars will bring to city dwellers, some urban developers are already designing infrastructure to accommodate this new technology. Perhaps the most dramatic change is that driverless cars will need fewer parking spaces. This is because self-driving cars would enable more people to share a single car, as the cars wouldn't have to sit in parking lots, they could drive themselves between different passengers. This could reduce the total number of cars on the road and the number of necessary parking spaces. Currently, developers in many cities are required to have a certain number of parking spaces on or near their properties. If they don't, they may have to pay a fine. This can be a problem for developers, especially in high-priced downtown areas. Having self-driving cars that can park themselves at a distance from high-priced properties could mean saving valuable real estate dollars. In anticipation of the widespread adoption of automated vehicles, companies in Los Angeles, California, and Nashville, Tennessee, are already creating developments with smaller parking areas that can eventually be converted to living spaces.

Researchers have found that eliminating the need to search for parking spots was valued very highly by urban citizens and might be a considerable factor in their purchase of a self-driving car. With the cars of today, people are often fighting for parking spaces as close to the doors as possible. "Our streets aren't designed for door-to-door service," planning expert Shannon McDonald said.[19] But self-driving cars could drop everybody off at the entrances, park any distance away where spots are available, and then pick up passengers upon receiving the signal to do so. This would eliminate wasted time and frustration over trying to find a good parking spot. According to Iglinski's research findings, "A typical car designed for private use is on average used for 50 to 60 minutes per day. Not only is it unproductive for 23 hours of parking but it also requires a few parking spaces. It is estimated that in cities there is six times more parking space assigned to each registered car than the vehicle takes up itself, which means that in developed countries with highly motorized societies, car parks take up approximately 15 percent of urban space, and in extreme cases as much as one third."[20] The time where cars would otherwise be sitting in a parking lot could be put to productive use by

> **WORDS IN CONTEXT**
>
> **rideshare**
>
> An arrangement in which a passenger travels in a private vehicle driven by its owner, for free or for a fee, especially as arranged on a website or app.

incorporating self-driving cars into **ridesharing** systems.

RIDESHARING

Another area where self-driving cars are sure to have a great impact is in ridesharing systems. In recent years, ridesharing companies such as Uber, Lyft, and Sidecar have grown immensely in popularity. These systems can operate in different ways. Riders can join a carpool or vanpool with other riders heading to similar, prearranged destinations, or they can summon a separate car to take them directly to wherever they need to go. Fees can either be paid during each ride, or they can be grouped together in an annual membership. Since the first ridesharing services debuted in 2012, the concept has proliferated around the world. Between 2012 and 2014, the number of ridesharing vehicles on the road grew 55 percent to more than 100,000, and the number of ridesharing members worldwide grew 65 percent to around 4.8 million. And the industry is expected to continue growing, with the number of ridesharing users projected to be at about 72.4 million in the United States alone by 2022. Part of the reason for this popularity is that ridesharing offers people the luxury and convenience of being in a private vehicle as opposed to public transportation while at the same time eliminating the costs of gas, insurance, and maintenance associated with car ownership.

In addition to these benefits to individuals, studies have found that ridesharing systems are beneficial to the large society in which they operate. Their use has been found to reduce the number of cars on the roads, which reduces harmful vehicle emissions. They have

Uber, a major ridesharing company, has started testing self-driving cars. Other ridesharing companies have also shown interest in eventually replacing their drivers with self-driving cars.

drastically impacted the way people travel, leading to declines in public transportation use and private car ownership. One North American study found that 25 percent of rideshare members postponed a new vehicle purchase and another 25 percent sold a car they already owned due to these services.

As automation technology matures, rideshare companies are looking at replacing their human drivers with self-driving cars. Lyft cofounder John Zimmer calls this shift "The Third Transportation Revolution," comparing self-driving cars to two other monumental shifts in transportation systems: railroad systems connecting communities in the nineteenth century and the invention of assembly line automobile production in the twentieth century.[21] Zimmer predicts that fully automated vehicles will conduct most of Lyft's rides by 2021 and that few people will privately own cars in the United States by 2025 because of the convenience and efficiency of these services. Removing the vehicles' drivers would result in lower operating expenses, leading to lower fees for users and creating even more competition with other transportation options.

The combination of ridesharing and automated vehicles is expected to decrease the number of cars on the road, which would reduce traffic congestion at any given time. Traffic congestion is usually a result of drivers collectively being inefficient in their use of the available road space. Humans are imperfect drivers. Habits of driving at inconsistent speeds, erratically merging, and attempting to swerve around fellow drivers to get ahead can all lead to a more inefficient use of the road than if the same number of cars were driving in an ideal traffic flow. This congestion can lead to more than just time wasted on the road. Traffic congestion cost drivers in the United States more than $300 billion in 2016. INRIX, a business firm that analyzes transportation systems, studied 1,064 cities in 2016 to discover the impact of current traffic conditions on everyday life. It found that Los Angeles had some of the worst traffic conditions. According to its findings, "the average driver in Los Angeles lost 104 hours last year while stuck in gridlock during the city's busy commuting times, as well as $2,408 on wasted fuel and productivity."[22] The US Department of Transportation (USDOT) conducted a similar study and reported that highway congestion costs each highway commuter in an urban area between $867 and $1,433 annually, depending on the size of the area. These are all costs that could be reduced if highway traffic could be streamlined with the use of self-driving cars.

ENVIRONMENTAL BENEFITS

Not only does traffic congestion affect individual drivers, it also takes a toll on the environment. In 2014, the USDOT reported that an average of 99.5 million gallons (376.6 million L) of fuel were wasted the previous year in very large urban areas due to traffic congestion alone. By reducing traffic, self-driving cars also have the potential to reduce harmful emissions and energy use. It has been estimated that the average passenger car releases about 5.2 tons (4.7 metric tons) of **carbon dioxide** into the atmosphere annually. This contributes to climate change. Studies indicate that if people were environmentally conscious while driving, they would be able to reduce their fuel consumption and harmful emissions by 10 to 20 percent. But the environment is often not at the forefront of drivers' minds, so they end up driving less efficiently and wasting valuable resources. However, self-driving cars could be programmed to always drive in a way that maximizes resources and creates as little waste as possible, thus saving that 10 to 20 percent in fuel consumption and emissions.

> **WORDS IN CONTEXT**
>
> **carbon dioxide**
> A colorless and nonflammable gas formed by the combustion of carbon-containing fuel such as petroleum and diesel.

FINANCIAL SAVINGS

The USDOT has also conducted extensive research on transportation expenditures. Its review of personal transportation expenses for 2016 found that Americans collectively spent more than $1 trillion on car-related costs. This includes the costs of purchasing motor vehicles as well as the related expenses of parts and accessories, repairs, rentals, gasoline and oil, parking fees, tolls, and insurance premiums. In 2015, researchers evaluated the reduction in costs that might result from using self-driving cars. They took into account reduced repair costs from fewer crashes, the reduction of travel time from less traffic congestion, and the savings in fuel and parking fees. They concluded the total annual savings for each vehicle would end up being between $2,000 and $4,000.

SAFETY

One of the greatest benefits of self-driving cars is their potential for improving roadway safety. In 2015, 2.4 million Americans were injured in highway transportation accidents. Of these, 1.4 million were the occupants of passenger cars, while the remaining injuries occurred among motorcyclists, truck or bus occupants, bicyclists, and pedestrians. Researchers and policymakers alike recognize the positive impact that self-driving cars could have on this issue. "Self-driving cars have the potential to save lives, especially when the majority of fatalities are caused by human error," US Representative Debbie Dingell of Michigan said in support of a bill designed to streamline safety regulations to help get self-driving cars on America's roads.[23]

Speeding and distracted driving have been found to be significant factors in many automobile accidents. The AAA Foundation for Traffic Safety conducted a study of teen drivers and found that distraction, including interacting with smartphones and talking to fellow passengers, was a factor in about six out of ten crashes. The study also discovered that speeding played a role in about 30 percent of fatal accidents.

Self-driving cars could be the much-needed solution to this deadly problem. They would help by eliminating human error, potentially reducing the number of crashes. Self-driving cars could eliminate the hazards of speeding, running stop signs and red lights, going

Some experts argue that, by eliminating human error, self-driving cars could reduce the number of car crashes. Self-driving cars could prevent speeding, distracted driving, and other human behaviors that are known to contribute to car accidents.

the wrong way on a one-way street, and distracted driving behaviors resulting from drowsiness, high emotions, or being under the influence of drugs or alcohol. One 2017 study by the Rand Corporation, based on current driving habits and crash data, projected that if self-driving vehicles dominated the roadways, around 600,000 lives could be saved from driving accidents by the year 2070 in the United States alone.

INCLUSIVITY

Self-driving cars could open up the door for more people to be able to travel independently than ever before. Currently, a significant portion of the population is unable to operate a motor vehicle due to age or disabilities. Self-driving cars would allow people with blindness or other disabilities a level of freedom of mobility currently unavailable to them. They could have their own private form of transportation rather than being forced to rely on public transportation or others to drive them.

Self-driving cars also create new possibilities for people who may be considered too young or too old to drive themselves. New drivers between the ages of sixteen and seventeen are three times more likely than adults to be part of a fatal car accident. Self-driving cars could make this age group's travels safer. And, with the right programming, self-driving could also allow children to ride in a car

DRIVING WITH DISABILITIES

Anil Lewis is the executive director of the National Federation of the Blind's Jernigan Institute, where he works to develop technology and services to improve life for people who are blind. Lewis, who is legally blind, notes that the technology to carry passengers who cannot see already exists; in fact, Google has already tested its driverless vehicles with people with blindness. However, what needs to be changed is the regulatory system as a whole, Lewis says. Currently, people must undergo a vision test to obtain a driver's license, which automatically excludes blind people from getting behind the wheel. Lewis is lobbying lawmakers to make changes to allow blind users to operate self-driving cars. "If it's designed correctly, if the vehicles are accessible . . . it's going to create an improved ability to travel that doesn't currently exist," Lewis said. Although there is still work to be done, self-driving cars have the potential to open up a whole new level of inclusivity to people with disabilities.

Quoted in Ryan Beene, "Blind 'Drivers' Step Up to Shape U.S. Push for Driverless Cars," Bloomberg Technology, July 2017. www.bloomberg.com.

on their own. Self-driving cars could also provide more mobility to older people. Transportation researcher Daniel Thomas explains, "Age takes a toll on vision, hearing, physical strength, and cognitive skills. Driving suffers as a result, with decreased reaction time and range of motion, and a decline in peripheral vision. Many older drivers recognize their diminishing driving skills. They limit their time on the road and drive when they feel the safest—avoiding rush hours, driving shorter distances, refraining from driving in poor weather or at night."[24] Self-driving cars could grant these older drivers more freedom to travel alone whenever they want.

Chapter 3

What Is the Negative Impact of Self-Driving Cars on Society?

Although self-driving cars appear to have a bright future, there are negative impacts. There are safety concerns associated with self-driving cars, and some people worry that society could become too reliant on automation. So, one of the biggest challenges facing self-driving cars is public acceptance. As of 2017, surveys have indicated that about 56 percent of people view self-driving cars with a positive opinion, 13.8 percent of people have negative concerns, and 29.4 percent have neutral views about the topic. According to transportation researcher Christopher Kohl, "Public acceptance is what will eventually determine when and how self-driving cars will actually be put to use, making it a crucial factor to take into consideration."[25]

SEEKING PUBLIC ACCEPTANCE

Studies have shown that people have a **bias** towards using their personal vehicles, even when this is not economically the best transportation option. Researchers have dubbed this phenomenon the "car effect." In one study, researchers posed different scenarios to the study participants. The scenarios involved choosing to take the subway, the bus, or a car in each circumstance. The study found that, "Although the average cost of taking a car ended up being about 50 percent more than taking the metro, people chose cars nearly two-to-one."[26] The study was theoretical and did not actually require people to have to ride (and deal with the consequences of) their chosen mode of transportation. The participants simply chose based on their preconceptions of each transportation mode. Although the actual results might vary slightly in the real world, researchers proved the point that people do have preconceived notions about various transportation options.

WORDS IN CONTEXT

bias
Favoring something, usually in a way that could be considered unfair.

Part of what fuels the public's resistance to self-driving cars is the fear of the unknown. This fear is further compounded when unexpected events and accidents occur in conjunction with the new technology. Researchers like Kohl believe that "unpredicted events and accidents that recently occurred with self-driving cars such as the first human casualty [a driver for Tesla who died using an autopilot feature] could lead to fear and reluctance to adopt."[27] Unless the technology of self-driving cars is introduced carefully and people are trained how to safely use it, it could pose significant dangers to those on the road.

AUTOMATION BIAS

One danger is that people could become reliant on automated driving technology to a fault, throwing common sense out the window as they let their machines do the thinking for them. Some critics claim that just because something can be automated does not mean that it should be automated. Engineering researcher Miltos Kyriakidis believes this because "humans tend to be poor supervisors of automation. Decades of research have shown that humans are not particularly good at tasks that require vigilance and sustained attention over long periods of time."[28] Yet this is exactly what monitoring a self-driving, or partially self-driving, car would require.

This is because of a phenomenon known as automation bias. Acclaimed technology writer Nicholas Carr explains, "Automation bias . . . creeps in when people give undue weight to the information coming through their monitors. Even when the information is wrong or misleading, they believe it. Their trust in the software becomes so strong that they ignore or discount other sources of information, including their own senses."[29] For example, when people blindly follow the directions of a faulty or outdated GPS system leading them around in circles, they are experiencing the results of automation bias. Another example is that people in large, four-wheel-drive vehicles may drive more recklessly than they otherwise would because they believe their vehicle will protect them from any danger. Although many

AUTOMATION BIAS IN ACTION

Automation bias is dangerous when driving because it can cause people to ignore environmental conditions or road signs which could lead them into hazardous situations. A harrowing example of automation bias occurred in 2008, when a Seattle school bus driver drove his 12-foot-high (3.7 m) bus, which happened to be full of students from a high school sports team, into a bridge with only a 9-foot-high clearance. The bridge shaved off the roof of the bus, and all twenty-one students were injured and hospitalized. When the driver was relating how this incident occurred, he told police that he had simply been following the instructions of his GPS. Trusting the GPS to keep him on the right track, he did not notice or heed the warning signs or lights that signaled the low bridge ahead.

technological innovations may make vehicles safer in theory, they might not have their intended results if they end up lulling people into a false sense of security.

ADDITIONAL SAFETY CONCERNS

Up to 93 percent of car crashes are the result of human error, and the great promise of self-driving cars is to remove human error. However, until all cars reach complete Level Five automation, people will still need to monitor self-driving car systems and be prepared to take action in an emergency. In fact, some studies have shown that a combination of human and automated drivers may actually result in an increased number of crashes because partially automated cars would have to contend with human errors, system errors, and the issue of switching back and forth between the two.

"Proving safety requires on-road and virtual testing to rigorously assess not only the technology but also the human interaction with automation," according to Kyriakidis.[30] Research suggests that the automated vehicle industry still needs to further study the awareness of human drivers when they are in a car but not actively driving. This would help the industry understand the behaviors of self-driving car users. Most automated vehicle testing has focused on the technology itself, and the testing of human interaction with the technology has mainly been limited to driving simulators. There is still much testing to be done in real-world driving scenarios before it can be determined that this technology is safe for the public to handle.

The issue of safety in self-driving cars is also involved when passengers have limitations that may hinder them from taking over in an emergency. People who are too young to drive, who are suffering from an illness or injury, or who live with a disability may be unable to safely take control of a malfunctioning car. They would be totally

People expect self-driving cars to provide convenience, as imagined in this image of a woman reading a book while her car drives on its own. However, there has been very little testing about how humans will interact with self-driving cars. Most testing so far has focused on the technology itself.

reliant on the self-driving technology. Even though these special circumstances requiring the human driver to take control may be rare, they are bound to arise, especially in the early stages of using this technology. According to Carr, "Many technical challenges remain to be met, such as navigating snowy or leaf-covered roads, dealing with unexpected detours, and interpreting the hand signals of traffic cops and road workers. Even the most powerful computers still have a hard time distinguishing a bit of harmless road debris (a flattened cardboard box, say) from a dangerous obstacle (a nail-studded chunk of plywood)."[31] Self-driving cars have great potential to be more inclusive to a wider variety of travelers. However, until the technology can be perfected to safely respond to emergency or unknown situations, caution needs to be taken when transporting passengers who may not be able to recognize and respond to these circumstances themselves.

POTENTIAL JOB LOSSES

It is not just the passengers of self-driving cars who may be in danger. Innovative technology, especially when it touches something as central to people's way of life as transportation, also threatens the status quo of the society in which it arises. The influential twentieth-century economist Joseph Schumpeter described innovation as "creative destruction"—a destructive process that challenges current best practices by superseding existing products or processes with new ones.[32] Self-driving car technology threatens the current balance of industry and infrastructure in our society. Jobs that involve human control of vehicles may be at risk. A technology program at the University of Oxford in England "recently predicted that computerization would eliminate nearly half the jobs in the US over the next 20 years," according to technology writer Benjamin Preston in February 2016.[33]

A wide variety of jobs involve driving. Human drivers are needed for taxis, buses, delivery trucks, and more. Some worry that these drivers could eventually lose their jobs to self-driving cars. Although some recent studies have found that potential job losses were ranked the least of people's many concerns about self-driving cars, this is still a significant issue for part of the population.

Millions of people's jobs could be affected. This includes taxi drivers, bus drivers, rideshare drivers, shipping truck drivers,

City bus drivers are one example of people whose jobs could eventually be replaced by self-driving cars. Labor unions have voiced concerns about this potential impact on the job market.

chauffeurs, and delivery drivers. Additionally, there are numerous support and maintenance jobs in the transportation industry that could be indirectly affected by the shift to self-driving cars. While self-driving cars would still require maintenance and repairs, many auto technicians who do not have a firm understanding of the cameras, sensors, and software powering self-driving cars may need to be retrained or replaced. Also, if self-driving cars successfully reduce the number of crashes, that may also reduce the need for auto mechanics overall.

The US Bureau of Labor Statistics reports around 160,000 Uber drivers, 160,000 transit bus drivers, 180,000 taxi drivers, and

500,000 school bus drivers could lose their jobs to self-driving cars. Approximately 2.4 million truckers and delivery drivers may have their jobs jeopardized as well. According to engineering researcher Hubert Iglinski, "propagation of AV (autonomous vehicles) will make millions of professional drivers lose their jobs, and finding new ones with low professional qualifications may prove to be a serious social problem."[34] Labor unions recognize this, and they have stressed the importance of lawmakers carefully considering the impact this technology could have on the current job market.

TRADITIONAL MANUFACTURING

In addition, the rise of self-driving cars inevitably means a disruption in the traditional automotive manufacturing industry, which, in 2015, was estimated to be valued at more than $1.6 trillion worldwide. According to Joel Barbier, a scholar from the Global Center for Digital Business Transformation, "We're already seeing a shift in value from traditional auto manufacturers to software and electronics companies, which will form the core of all automotive systems. Traditional parts manufacturers will face competition from more technology-focused companies."[35] Barbier also notes, "By 2030, [consulting firm PricewaterhouseCoopers] predicts electronics will account for 50 percent of automobile manufacturing costs."[36] Additionally, Preston notes that "Annual auto sales in the United States could decline by as much as 40 percent, and there would be a 60-percent drop in the total number of vehicles on the road. Driverless vehicles, using the same sort of technology that today connects Uber drivers with people needing rides, could be used to their maximum potential instead of sitting idle most of the time, as the majority of vehicles do today. . . . Ford and GM, which have factories all over North America, will have to cut production by more than half as conventional vehicles cede the roads to autonomous ones."[37] With the potential to introduce self-driving cars for certain functions, such as public transportation, as early as 2020, the automotive and transportation industry is in for a huge adjustment.

ECONOMY AND INFRASTRUCTURE

City economies are sure to be impacted by self-driving cars as well. In 2015, Americans spent $23 billion on parking fees and tolls. But self-driving cars could be programmed to avoid parking in expensive spots, which could decrease cities' revenue from parking fees. Self-driving cars could also be programmed to avoid no-parking zones and to leave a parking meter once the meter has expired. The revenue that cities get from parking fees and tolls is generally put toward public services. According to Preston, "Researchers at the Brookings Institute point out that a driverless fleet obeying the letter of the law will cut into the billions that miscreants currently pay into public coffers. . . . In 2013, smartphone-operated parking meters, while good for consumers, led to a $6 million decrease in ticket revenue in Washington, D.C., alone. It's not impossible to rethink taxes and fees, but establishing new ones when old ones are obsolete is a difficult political undertaking. Not many voters favor new taxes or fees, even if the old ones have gone away."[38] To recoup this income, cities may begin implementing additional fees, such as fees for when vehicles pass through certain areas at peak traffic hours.

The very infrastructure of cities will also be affected by self-driving cars. Automobiles have long been accused of destroying the rural fabric of American society. Indeed, when automobiles were first introduced, people living in rural communities, as well as those living in cities, suddenly had access to a much greater area in which to live everyday life. This opened up new possibilities for people, but it also, inevitably, altered the culture of their local communities.

Self-driving cars could be programmed to avoid parking meters, toll booths, and other places that require payment for parking or driving. Experts say this could negatively affect cities that rely on those sources of income.

Researchers Adam Stocker and Susan Shaheen wrote, "Any new transportation service introduced into an ecosystem of existing travel options will have impacts on subsequent travel behavior of the users of the new system."[39] These changes in travel behavior may include people moving farther away from their workplaces due to the productive time gained commuting in a self-driving car. Zoning experts believe that self-driving cars could directly influence the way housing developments and cities are planned. Real estate writer Patrick Sisson says, "The convergence of three new technologies—automation, electrification, and shared mobility—has the potential to create a whole new wave of automation-induced sprawl without proper planning and regulation."[40] The phenomenon of **urban sprawl** could cause real estate prices to fluctuate and change the way that real estate is developed. But self-driving cars will likely have the biggest impact on parking spaces and streets.

> **WORDS IN CONTEXT**
>
> **urban sprawl**
> The rapid and uncontrolled expansion of developments such as housing and shopping centers away from a central urban point. This is also called suburbanization.

As of 2017, there were approximately 263 million cars on US roads, requiring around 2 billion parking spaces to accommodate them. Because passenger cars need to be able to park close enough for their drivers to be within walking distance of each of their destinations, there are around eight parking spaces for each car in most cities. Self-driving cars, which are more likely to be continually driving or to park themselves back at home after dropping off their passengers, may require fewer parking spaces, prompting the unused spaces to be redeveloped for other uses. Additionally, roads take up a valuable 25 to 35 percent of the average city's land area. Some of these roads may have to be fixed, rerouted, or otherwise updated to better support the self-driving cars traveling on them. While the reduction of land space devoted to roads and parking may be beneficial in the long run, the transition to reach that point is sure to be tumultuous for the people living and working near the affected roads and parking lots. It will also be extremely expensive for the governments and private companies responsible for these infrastructure updates. No one knows exactly how self-driving cars will affect cities, but it is clear that they will have an impact. According to Sisson, "It's definitely time to

Although self-driving cars are expected to eliminate human error, the cameras, sensors, and other technologies on the cars are bound to malfunction. More testing is needed to see how glitches in the technology should be handled.

start looking at the many land-use issues this technology will leave in its wake."[41]

MAINTENANCE AND MALFUNCTIONS

Cost is another negative impact of self-driving cars. Maintenance and repair of self-driving cars is likely to be expensive. It's also likely that there will be malfunctions in making and repairing self-driving cars. According to Carr, "Machines share the fallibility of their makers. Sooner or later, even the most advanced technology will break

With all of the technology inside self-driving cars, experts say malfunctions are inevitable. Companies are working to improve the technology and reduce the potential for dangerous glitches.

down, misfire, or, in the case of a computerized system, encounter a cluster of circumstances that its designers and programmers never anticipated and that leave its algorithms baffled."[42]

Even with planes, which have proven to be easier to safely automate than cars, it is not unusual for pilots to step in to handle bad weather, mechanical glitches, and other unusual circumstances. In fact, experience from the aviation industry has shown that automating vehicles might create more problems than it solves. This is because, in the words of Carr, "All the parts may work flawlessly, but a small error or oversight in system design—a glitch that might be buried in hundreds of thousands of lines of software code—can still cause a major accident."[43] Even if it were possible to create perfect self-driving technology, this technology would always be operating in an imperfect environment with unforeseen and unpredictable circumstances. As self-driving car technology will be new to most people as it is introduced, the drivers-turned-passengers may be woefully unprepared for how to handle the vehicle and keep themselves safe in the case of an emergency, which could open up a whole new world of possibilities for injuries and liability.

HACKING

Related to the issue of malfunctions is the issue of **hacking**. As computers inevitably become more interconnected with self-driving cars, the possibility to move from hacking one item to a whole network of items increases. The hacking might stem from criminals trying to gain profit, terrorists wishing to cause fear and turmoil, or simply individuals looking for a thrill. Hacking could enable others to take control of a vehicle or install viruses that could be transmitted between cars. Although hacking attacks on any technology can have serious consequences, the risk is especially severe with self-driving cars because the passengers' safety could be put in jeopardy.

> **WORDS IN CONTEXT**
>
> **hacking**
> Using a computer to gain unauthorized access to data in a system.

Andy Greenberg, senior writer on technology and hacking issues, participated in an experiment in which he drove a standard Jeep Cherokee down the highway. While he was traveling at 70 mph (113 km/h), various functions were enabled in the car, completely unbidden by him. He writes, "Though I hadn't touched the dashboard, the vents in the Jeep Cherokee started blasting cold air at the

Experts say the technology in self-driving cars will likely be vulnerable to hackers. However, studies have shown that the more experience people have with driverless cars, the less fearful they are of privacy issues surrounding the technology.

maximum setting, chilling the sweat on my back through the in-seat climate control system. Next the radio switched to the local hip-hop station and began blaring Skee-lo at full volume. I spun the control knob left and hit the power button, to no avail. Then the windshield wipers turned on, and wiper fluid blurred the glass."[44] The hackers, who were also participants in the experiment, went as far as to disable the accelerator while Greenberg was in the middle of a busy interstate. All of this was accomplished remotely through an Internet-connected feature in the car. At the time of the experiment, the researchers estimated there were around 471,000 vehicles on the road with similar vulnerabilities, a number that can only increase with the proliferation of highly computerized self-driving cars.

However, studies have shown that people who are already using automated technology in their cars have fewer concerns about hacking and privacy than those who are not. According to researcher Michael König, "This leads to the conclusion that prior experience with automated features could raise drivers' trust in automation. A step-by-step advancement of 'driver assistance' systems together with a widespread inclusion of such features in today's cars could thus steadily grow peoples' trust in automation."[45] In other words, the solution of overcoming privacy and hacking concerns about self-driving cars could lie in slowly introducing more and more automated features to build up trust, allowing the drivers of the vehicles to feel in control until they are confident enough in the technology to accept it. However, regardless of public acceptance, there is still work to be done to make driverless vehicles safer from the threat of hacking.

Chapter 4

What Is the Future of Self-Driving Cars?

Automobile technology has been evolving since it was first introduced around the beginning of the twentieth century. It has evolved to encompass modern self-driving car technology. Vehicles with Level Two, Level Three, and even Level Four automation can now be found on city streets around the world. Experts have predicted that over the following decades, high-level automation will become more widespread. The race is on to develop, test, and release Level Five automated vehicles.

People have envisioned a future with fully self-driving, Level Five automated vehicles for many years. This futuristic concept was initially shown in movies and other entertainment media, and modern technology is bringing the idea closer to reality. It would be an idealistic future in which cars could essentially work for their owners by running errands for them or driving their commutes. Self-driving cars could even bring in some extra money for their owners by providing rides to other people when the cars are not in use by their owners. But the applications of self-driving technology stretch far beyond personal use. Entirely automated public transportation systems could improve commutes for people who don't own their own vehicles. Mass transit bus systems as well as taxi companies, rideshare systems, and carpooling networks could all operate with the freedom of not requiring drivers.

The company Tesla has released electric cars with some self-driving features. Private companies, including Tesla, are leading the way when it comes to researching and developing self-driving cars.

Private businesses could also reap the benefits of self-driving car technology by using the cars for shipping and deliveries, mapping and data gathering, and mobile advertising. Finally, public services such as police, fire, ambulance, and other emergency and patrol vehicles could help keep communities safer without having to rely on drivers. Although the possibilities for self-driving cars are practically endless, there are several important issues—including costs, legislation, privacy, liability, and ethical questions—that need to be addressed before this highly automated future can become a reality.

OVERCOMING THE COSTS

The price of self-driving cars, including the initial purchase price and later maintenance expenses, may decrease as time goes on and the technology becomes more popular. But for now, self-driving cars are expected to be quite expensive when they are first introduced to the marketplace. This high cost could be a major hindrance to the widespread development and public acceptance of self-driving cars. Experts predict that Level Four self-driving car technology will add anywhere between $10,000 and $50,000 to the price of an equivalent nonautomated car. According to engineering researcher Hubert Iglinski, "The cost of purchase of an AV is currently very high—on average 4-5 times higher than of a typical car purchased in the USA. . . . Therefore, it is difficult to imagine that in the future many people could afford to buy AV and then, for 95 percent of the time, leave them idle at car parks."[46]

As far as people actually being willing to pay for self-driving car technology, a 2016 study revealed, "The average household is willing to pay a significant amount for automation: about $3,500 for partial automation and $4,900 for full automation."[47] However, they also noted that there was a significant split in the population they studied. Out of the surveyed 1,260 individuals, "a significant share of the sample is willing to pay above $10,000 for full automation technology while many are not willing to pay any positive amount for the technology."[48] In other words, part of the population is willing to pay a significant amount for self-driving cars, while the remaining portion of the population is willing to pay little to nothing extra at all. Traditionally, when new products or technologies are introduced to the marketplace, they face both early and late adopters. Although not everyone is ready to jump onboard with self-driving cars right away, a few **early adopters** of the technology can go a long way in demonstrating its benefits as the rest

WORDS IN CONTEXT

early adopter
Someone who starts using a product or technology as soon as it becomes available.

of the market catches on. It is a good sign that there is a fairly even split in consumer opinions of self-driving cars currently, as that means there are plenty of people to set examples to those who are more hesitant about the change.

The early adopters are likely to be people who already have highly automated features in their vehicle or, at the other end of the spectrum, people who currently do not drive a car at all. Based on his study regarding the resistance of potential users to self-driving cars, researcher Michael König explains, "People currently not possessing a car thus might have viewed self-drive technology as an opportunity to again (or even for the first time) participate in car traffic, while people who had experienced well-functioning automated features in their present cars might have had a higher acceptance due to their higher level of trust in the technology. In contrast, people with limited or no automation in their current vehicles could have tended to be more wary given their unfamiliarity with advanced automation technology."[49]

Although segments of the population are showing interest in self-driving cars, this does not necessarily mean that the technology will be adopted right away. Some other advances in transportation technology and systems have found difficulty being accepted by commuters. Some examples are **electric cars** and ridesharing networks. These things have been available for several years and are familiar to the general public, but people overwhelmingly prefer driving their own gasoline-powered cars. Although some people certainly take

> **WORDS IN CONTEXT**
>
> **electric car**
>
> Electric cars or EVs (electric vehicles) are powered exclusively by energy stored in rechargeable batteries, which are recharged using electricity.

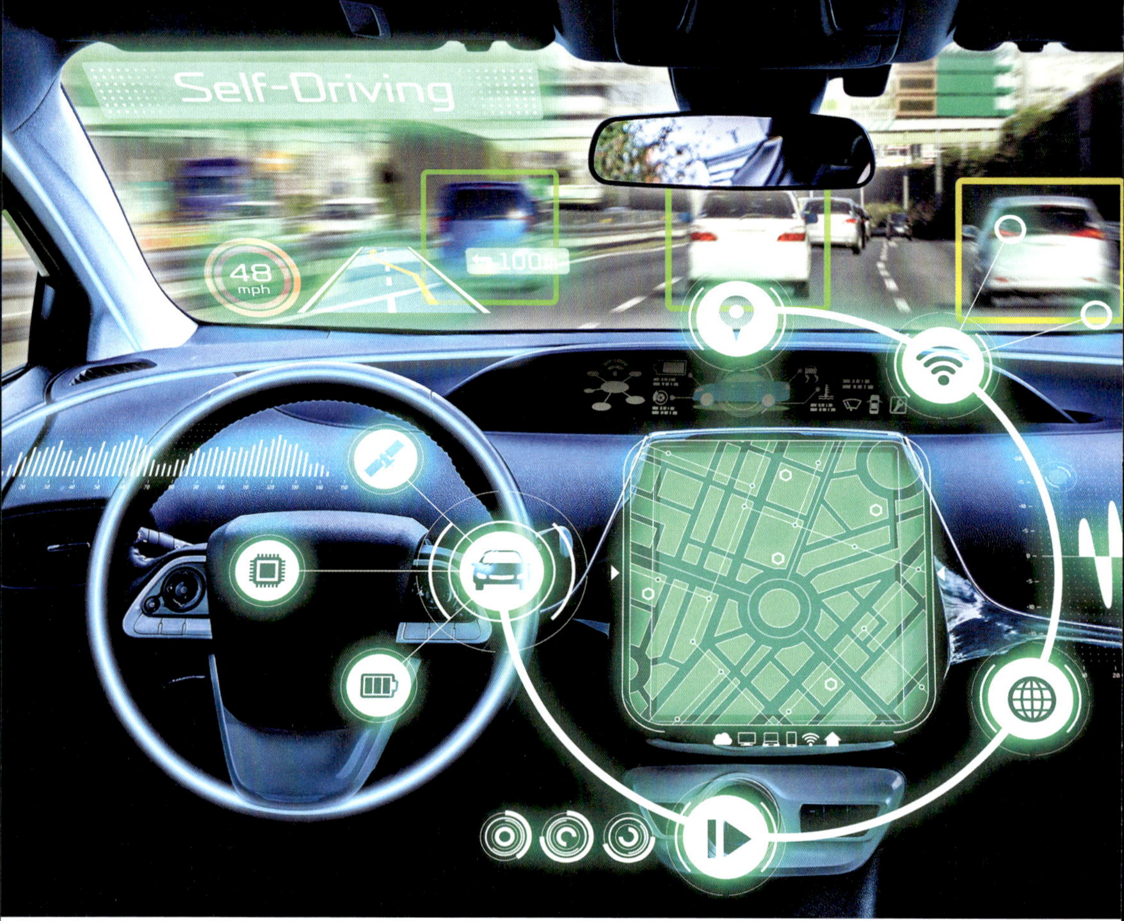

Laws and regulations for testing self-driving cars have varied from state to state. New York and California are two states that have approved plans to allow some level of testing on public roads.

advantage of these more efficient options, for the most part, they are underutilized.

NEW LEGISLATION

As major automakers have taken significant steps in developing self-driving cars, lawmakers have started working to help put self-driving cars on the roads. In September 2017, US Congress discussed a bill that would enable hundreds of thousands of self-driving cars to drive on public roads over the following few years. Automotive industry leaders Ford, General Motors, and Waymo backed the bill. The legislation is significant because it offers self-driving car manufacturers some exemptions to standard safety regulations for components including brakes, steering, and airbags. Despite this freedom, automakers would still need to comply with other safety standards from the National Highway Traffic Safety Administration (NHTSA).

While this bill holds great promise for the self-driving car industry and encourages experimental development of self-driving cars, the bill is not without its critics. Some say that it could allow for weaker standards for airbag, braking, and steering systems. "This bill threatens the safety of the American public because it will give automakers a huge number of exemptions for safety standards for no reason at all but because they want their autonomous vehicles to be first on the lot," said Joan Claybrook, a chairwoman of Advocates for Highway and Auto Safety. "This is totally reckless."[50] Automakers have replied to the critics of safety standards, claiming that it does not make sense to apply vehicle safety laws designed for traditional vehicles to driverless vehicles. Additionally, lobbyists for the automotive industry have praised the bill, saying that it will allow the NHTSA to standardize driverless car safety rules throughout the nation. By early 2018, the bill had not been passed into law.

With no encompassing federal law to regulate self-driving cars, the self-driving car industry has mostly been regulated by state laws. These laws vary widely from state to state. The NHTSA has sought to standardize the manufacturing and regulation of self-driving cars across the country. This could help get self-driving cars on the roads faster. As researchers Adam Stocker and Susan Shaheen explain, "[The] NHTSA released their Federal Automated Vehicles Policy that intends to establish a foundation and framework for regulation of AVs in the US, and it outlines a proposed fifteen-point safety checklist. The fifteen-point certification list includes regulatory recommendations covering topics such as: safety, data sharing, privacy, cybersecurity, and ethical considerations, among other topics. The document serves as a starting point for recommendations and guidance rather than concrete rulemaking in order to speed the delivery of an initial regulatory framework."[51]

While the NHTSA's efforts show that policymakers are starting to pay attention to self-driving cars, local and state governments have some critiques of this federal control, which prevents them from passing certain local laws related to self-driving cars. Essentially, the proposed federal legislation would allow local governments to determine licensing, insurance, and transportation safety laws related to self-driving cars, as they do with traditional cars, but it would prevent state governments from passing their own laws relating to how the cars are designed and operated. The NHTSA and the US Department of Transportation, which regulate development of self-driving car software, have taken significant steps forward, but there is still work to do to standardize and regulate self-driving car technology.

In addition to putting policies in place to standardize safety features, driving laws also need to be revised to accommodate automated vehicles. In 2011, Nevada was the first state—and the first place in the world—to allow self-driving cars on public roads. State officials worked closely with Google, which wanted to use Nevada's long, clear highways to test its automated cars. By 2017, Washington DC as well as eight states—Nevada, California, Florida, Louisiana, Michigan, North Dakota, Tennessee, and Utah—had legislation or executive orders relating to self-driving cars.

Self-driving cars are equipped with cameras and other technologies that collect data. Some people worry about how people's privacy will be protected amid this technology.

PRIVACY STANDARDS

In addition to safety and traffic regulations, laws relating to privacy for the owners of self-driving cars will need to be established. As electronics become increasingly connected to the Internet and to each other, the potential for breaches in privacy become more prevalent. Cars' reliance on computerized systems and connectivity increases with each level of automation, and concerns about privacy are pervasive even with today's vehicles with lower levels of automation. Due to worries about personal privacy, GPS tracking, especially in rental vehicles, has been a point of debate for some, while others are more focused on data collection by the vehicle manufacturers themselves. Video cameras on traffic signals and sensors in toll zones that collect driver information have also prompted privacy concerns.

While some lobbyists push for more governmental control of the way auto companies track user data, others argue that this would not be effective in preserving personal privacy. They believe it would be better to allow things to be interconnected and, essentially, allow anyone to know anything rather than turning a blind eye to inevitable privacy issues. The past and future travel data stored in the computer systems of increasingly intelligent autonomous vehicles could be used for a wide range of purposes from marketing to law enforcement. König said, "by tracking peoples' daily driving, predictability of where those people will go in the future can be maximized up to 93 percent, given that self-driving cars could be tracked steadily involving vehicle location, as well as information about where the user wanted to go, did go, and what the user could have seen along the way."[52]

In order to help mitigate these concerns, the state of California has regulations stating that the "manufacturer of the autonomous technology installed on a vehicle shall provide a written disclosure to the purchaser of an autonomous vehicle that describes what information is collected by the autonomous technology equipped on the vehicle."[53] Although California is taking some measures to protect people's privacy, the state also requires that self-driving cars preserve detailed information about what the vehicle was doing in the 30 seconds before it experiences an accident. This requirement is to help determine the fault in an accident.

It is important to understand that there will be a tradeoff between how private a self-driving vehicle is and how connected and "smart" it is. If the owners of self-driving cars have complete control over their vehicles, storing maps and other data necessary for the car to run onboard, they will inevitably have more freedom and privacy than if the vehicles are connected to a network of cars or partially controlled or powered by some outside source, such as smart roads. Additionally, any technology that allows self-driving cars to communicate with one another has the potential to compromise its users' privacy. According to automotive researcher Jack Boeglin, "The degree to which communicative vehicles affect their users' privacy will be determined in large part by the ongoing national debate over location privacy. Importantly, federal courts have yet to indicate decisively when an individual's location data can be accessed by law enforcement and how it can be used."[54] The results of this decision can have a huge impact on how on private self-driving cars are developed.

ETHICAL QUESTIONS

Just as certain standards relating to privacy need to be agreed upon before self-driving cars are ready to hit the road, there are a few questions of **ethics** that need to be sorted out for the vehicles themselves. New York University psychology professor Gary Marcus noted that the arrival of self-driving cars would mark the start of a new era in which machines will have to have "ethical systems."[55] Until recently, consideration of the morals of machines and robots had mainly been limited to philosophical discussions or science-fiction stories. Technology writer Nicholas Carr explains: "Ethical considerations have often influenced the design of tools—guns have safeties, motors have governors, search engines have filters—but machines haven't been required to have consciences.

WORDS IN CONTEXT

ethics
Moral principles that govern someone's behavior and activities.

ETHICAL CONSIDERATIONS FOR SELF-DRIVING CARS

An example of an ethical problem that a self-driving car would likely encounter is having to react to a dog wandering in front of the vehicle on an icy road. Carr presents such a problem: "If [the car's] algorithms calculate that hitting the brakes would give the dog a 53 percent chance of survival but would entail an 18 percent chance of damaging the car and a 4 percent chance of causing injury to you, does it conclude that trying to save the animal would be the right thing to do? How does the software, working on its own, translate a set of numbers into a decision that has both practical and moral consequences?" The issue would be further complicated if the car were to recognize the animal as a neighbor's, or even the car owner's, pet. What's more, it could be a person wandering into the street. What if swerving to try to save them would have the potential to cause harm to the passengers in that car and the passengers in the lane of oncoming traffic? Would the computers in the cars be able to calculate how to react appropriately to those situations? Although a perfect solution may never be reached, these are difficult questions that need to be considered before self-driving cars are ready to hit the roads.

Quoted in Nicholas Carr, *The Glass Cage: Automation and Us*. New York: W. W. Norton & Company, Inc., 2014, p. 184.

> They haven't had to adjust their own operation in real time to account for the ethical vagaries of a situation. . . . As robots and computers become more adept at sensing the world and acting autonomously in it, they'll inevitably face situations in which there's no one right choice. . . . It's impossible to automate complex human activities without also automating moral choices."[56]

Although the computers in self-driving cars would certainly be able to weigh many possible options and consequences more efficiently than human drivers, they, like humans, are not without flaws.

One of the biggest problems is that there is no set of ethical rules that everyone agrees upon, something that philosophers have unsuccessfully been trying to achieve for centuries. Philosophy writer Olivia Goldhill relates the ethical issues sure to be encountered by self-driving cars to what is known as the Trolley Problem. It describes a trolley careening down the tracks towards five pedestrians. The trolley could be diverted, but doing so would actively put an individual who is on the other track in danger. Goldhill writes, "Is it morally acceptable to kill one to save five, or should you allow five to die rather than actively hurt one? Though the Trolley Problem sounds farfetched, autonomous vehicles will be unable to avoid comparable scenarios. If a car is in a situation where any action will put either the car passenger or someone else in danger—if there's a truck crash ahead and the only options are to swerve into a motorbike or off a cliff—then how should the car be programmed to respond?"[57]

These are scenarios that philosophers and software developers alike are testing and working into the programming of self-driving cars. Carr believes: "If autonomous machines are to be set loose in the world, moral codes will have to be translated, however imperfectly, into software codes."[58] However, the questions still remain, could the conclusion reached by an algorithm still be the same as one reached by a human decision? And would this decision be right?

LIABILITY AND INSURANCE

As self-driving cars become widespread, they will create new issues for the insurance industry. In normal cars, the driver is generally liable for the actions he or she takes behind the wheel. But who or what is responsible when an automated car causes an accident? If a person behind the wheel could have taken control, some believe he or she should be liable. Others believe the manufacturers of the vehicles or even a government entity should take ultimate responsibility for crashes, as the purpose of having a self-driving car is to take those responsibilities away from the human driver. If there were an obvious defect in design or software functioning, it would make sense for the manufacturers to be held liable. Manufacturers should be held responsible for circumstances leading to an accident that the car should have clearly foreseen, but they cannot be expected to foresee every possible scenario. In the case of a unique or unforeseeable danger, the user would still be responsible.

In some visions of the self-driving future, cars would operate more as part of a network rather than as individual, private vehicles. In this scenario, in which automated vehicles offer users little control, liability could not fall on the users or manufacturers. It would have to fall on the government or whatever entity is controlling the automated roadway systems. Alternatively, a market share approach could be taken where, according to Boeglin, "AV manufacturers could be held liable according to their market share for accidents involving nondiscretionary communicative vehicles. . . . In effect, each manufacturer would contribute to a fund from which victims would be compensated without having to prove responsibility for any accidents."[59]

In any event, these messy questions regarding liability and self-driving cars will require more flexibility than what is currently allowed by the traditional liability framework. The entire automobile insurance industry will need to be revamped in order to accommodate self-driving cars. Some insurance companies have already started down this road by offering discounts when cars have certain types of automated technology, such as autonomous cruise control or electronic stability control. It's likely that insurance companies will continue monitoring the development of self-driving car technology.

Many legal issues are sure to arise as self-driving car technology continues to develop. Liability is one issue, as it may not be clear who is liable in a car crash involving a fully automated car.

SHIFTING ATTITUDES

There is clearly a long road to travel before the idealized vision of self-driving cars can become a reality. However, significant progress has been made over the last few decades. There was pushback when the automobile was first introduced to society, so it should come as no surprise that there has been some amount of resistance with new self-driving car technology as well. But researchers have already seen this resistance start to decrease. It is expected that self-driving cars will continue to gain public acceptance as the technology becomes more familiar and less expensive.

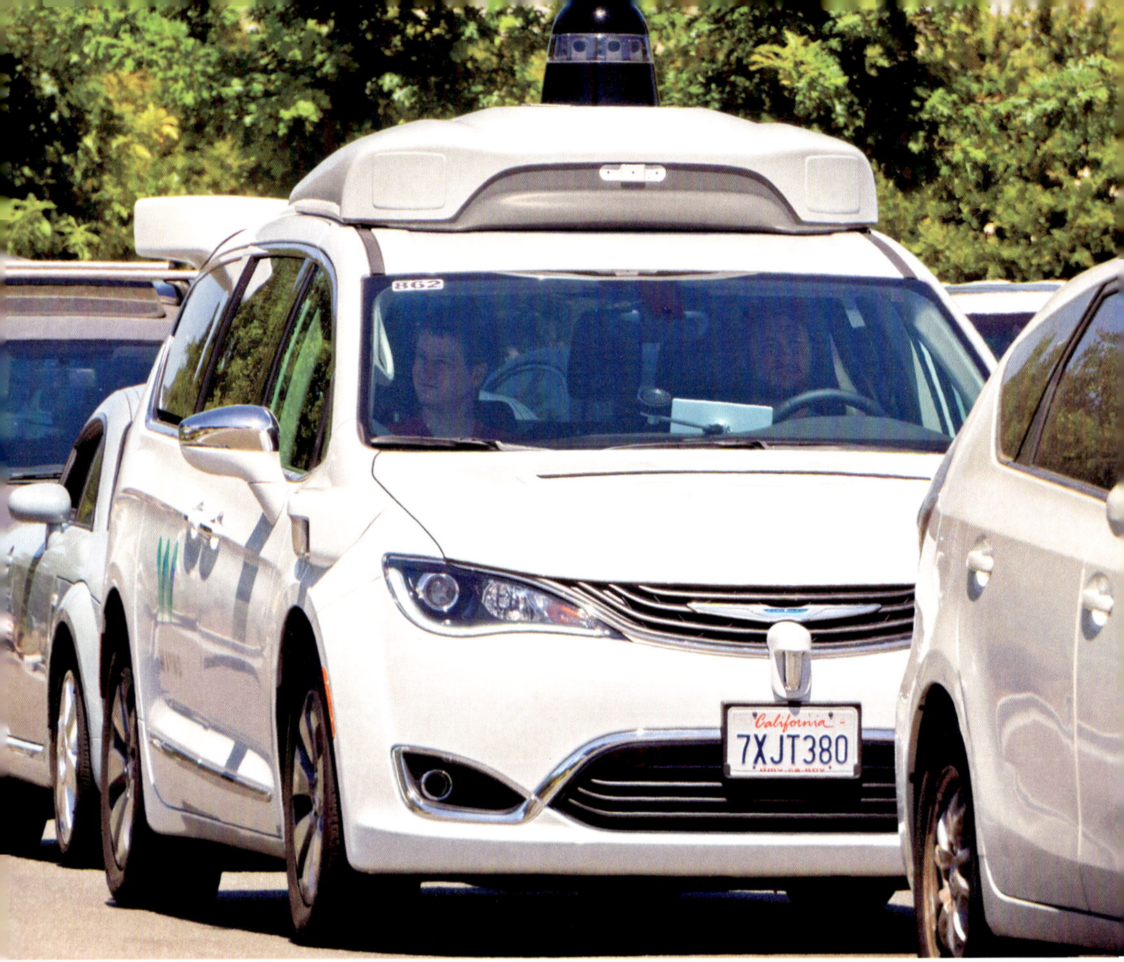

As the technology of self-driving cars continues to be developed and tested, experts warn that companies should listen to consumers. Despite remaining questions about this technology, self-driving cars are expected to provide many benefits in the future.

Kohl notes that "an overestimation of benefits might lead to misuse of self-driving cars, disappointment of initial users, and can have fatal consequences. Underestimation or not even recognizing benefits on the developer side could lead to self-driving cars that do not exploit their full potential. An overestimation of risks by the public could lead to resistance against self-driving cars before they even become publicly available."[60] With the issue of introducing self-driving cars to consumers, balance is key. A moderate and steady integration of automated features assimilated into the technology already being used will help people become familiar and comfortable with self-driving technology. Exaggeration in either direction, blowing the dangers out of proportion or overestimating the benefits, can scare potential consumers away or lead to disappointment, ultimately leading to further setbacks in winning over public opinion. However, if developers carefully respond to consumers' needs, the self-driving car will eventually be in a position to shape society.

Self-driving cars are a significant development in technology with the power to change society dramatically. Therefore, it is important to consider not only the exciting possibilities but also the challenges that their introduction to society will inevitably carry. Because technology is continually shaping and reshaping human behavior, we will not understand the full impact of self-driving cars until after they are here. However, by looking back at automotive history as well as examining the automated features that are already common in the cars of today, society can prepare to embrace self-driving cars and the changes that accompany them.

Source Notes

Introduction: Self-Driving Cars Today

1. Adam Stocker and Susan Shaheen, "Shared Automated Vehicles: Review of Business Models," *International Transport Forum*, 2017, www.itf-oecd.org.

2. M. Konig and L. Neumayr, "Users' Resistance Towards Radical Innovations: The Case of the Self-Driving Car," *Elsevier Transportation Research Part F*, vol. 44, no. 42-52, 2017, p. 1.

3. Quoted in Jon Walker, "The Self-Driving Car Timeline – Predictions from the Top 11 Global Automakers," *TechEmergence*, August 24, 2018. www.techemergence.com.

4. "Summon Tesla from Your Phone," Tesla, January 10, 2016. www.tesla.com.

5. M. Kyriakidis, "A Human Factors Perspective on Automated Driving," *Theoretical Issues in Ergonomics Science*, March 8, 2017, p. 1.

6. Quoted in Patrick Sisson, "As Self-Driving Cars Hit the Road, Real Estate Development May Take New Direction," *Curbed.com,* May 16, 2017. www.curbed.com.

Chapter 1: What Is the Technology Behind Self-Driving Cars?

7. Gautam Shroff, *The Intelligent Web*. New York: Oxford University Press, 2013, p. 239.

8. National Highway Traffic Safety Administration, "Vehicle-to-Vehicle Communications for Safety," www.nhtsa.gov.

9. Quoted in Chaim Gartenberg, "Wireless vehicle-to-vehicle communication would be required in new cars under proposed DOT rule," *The Verge,* December 13, 2016. www.theverge.com.

10. Quoted in Paul A. Eisenstein, "When 'smart cars' meet 'smart roads' bumpers may bump less," *The Christian Science Monitor*, 1988. www.csmonitor.com.

11. Jake Lingeman, "The 6 Levels of Autonomous Driving: Autoweek Explains," *Autoweek,* September 25, 2017. www.autoweek.com.

12. Alex Davies, "An Oral History of the DARPA Grand Challenge, the Grueling Robot Race that Launched the Self-Driving Car," *Wired*, August 3, 2017. www.wired.com.

13. Quoted in Sharon Weinberger, *The Imagineers of War*. New York: Alfred A. Knopf, 2017, p. 320.

14. Joseph Hooper, "From DARPA Grand Challenge 2004 DARPA's Debacle in the Desert," *Popular Science*, June 4, 2004. www.popsci.com.

15. Hooper, "From DARPA Grand Challenge 2004 DARPA's Debacle in the Desert."

16. Quoted in Weinberger, *The Imagineers of War*. p. 332.

Chapter 2: What Is the Positive Impact of Self-Driving Cars on Society?

17. Quoted in Tamra Johnson, "Americans Spend an Average of 17,600 Minutes Driving Each Year," *AAA NewsRoom*, September 8, 2016. newsroom.aaa.com.

18. Hubert Iglinski and Maciej Babiak, "Analysis of the Potential of Autonomous Vehicles in Reducing the Emissions of Greenhouse Gases in Road Transport," *Elsevier Procedia Engineering*, vol. 192, no. 353-358, 2017.

19. Quoted in Sisson, "As Self-Driving Cars Hit the Road, Real Estate Development May Take New Direction."

20. Iglinski and Babiak, "Analysis of the Potential of Autonomous Vehicles in Reducing the Emissions of Greenhouse Gases in Road Transport."

21. Socker and Shaheen, "Shared Automated Vehicles: Review of Business Models."

22. Quoted in Zamira Rahim, "Here's How Much Sitting in Traffic is Costing You," *Time*, February 21, 2017. www.time.com.

23. Quoted in Cecilia Kang, "Self-Driving Cars' Prospects Rise With Vote by House," *New York Times*, September 6, 2017. www.nytimes.com.

24. Quoted in Kaitlen J. Exum and Lynn M. Messina, *The Car and Its Future*. New York: H. W. Wilson Company, 2004, p. 62.

Chapter 3: What Is the Negative Impact of Self-Driving Cars on Society?

25. Christopher Kohl, "Disruption of Individual Mobility Ahead? A Longitudinal Study of Risk and benefit Perceptions of Self-Driving Cars of Twitter," Technical University of Munich, Department of Informatics, 2017, p. 1221.

26. Quoted in Eric Jaffe, "Why People Choose Cars, Even When Mass Transit Would Serve Them Better," *CityLab*, February 1, 2013. www.citylab.com.

27. Kohl, "Disruption of Individual Mobility Ahead? A Longitudinal Study of Risk and Benefit Perceptions of Self-Driving Cars of Twitter." p. 1220.

28. Kyriakidis, "A Human Factors Perspective on Automated Driving," *Theoretical Issues in Ergonomics Science*. p. 4.

29. Nicholas Carr, *The Glass Cage: Automation and Us*. New York: W. W. Norton & Company, Inc., 2014. p. 69.

30. Kyriakidis, "A Human Factors Perspective on Automated Driving," *Theoretical Issues in Ergonomics Science*. p. 10–12.

31. Carr, *The Glass Cage: Automation and Us*. p. 70.

32. Konig and Neumayr, "Users' Resistance Towards Radical Innovations: The Case of the Self-Driving Car." p. 43.

Source Notes Continued

33. Benjamin Preston, "Autonomy's Roadkill: The Path to Driverless Cars Will Be Strewn with the Carcasses of Big Industry," *Car and Driver* (blog), February 26, 2016. blog.caranddriver.com.

34. Iglinski and Babiak, "Analysis of the Potential of Autonomous Vehicles in Reducing the Emissions of Greenhouse Gases in Road Transport."

35. Joel Barbier, "Self-Driving Cars Will Disrupt More Than the Auto Industry. Here Are the Winners and Losers," *CNBC.com*, May 3, 2017. www.cnbc.com.

36. Barbier, "Self-driving cars will disrupt more than the auto industry. Here are the winners and losers."

37. Preston, "Autonomy's Roadkill: The Path to Driverless Cars Will Be Strewn with the Carcasses of Big Industry."

38. Preston, "Autonomy's Roadkill: The Path to Driverless Cars Will Be Strewn with the Carcasses of Big Industry."

39. Socker and Shaheen, "Shared Automated Vehicles: Review of Business Models."

40. Quoted in Sisson, "As Self-Driving Cars Hit the Road, Real Estate Development May Take New Direction."

41. Quoted in Sisson, "As Self-Driving Cars Hit the Road, Real Estate Development May Take New Direction."

42. Carr, *The Glass Cage: Automation and Us*.

43. Carr, *The Glass Cage: Automation and Us*. p. 158.

44. Andy Greenberg, "Hackers Remotely Kill a Jeep on the Highway—With Me In It," *Wired*, July 21, 2015. www.wired.com.

45. Konig and Neumayr, "Users' Resistance Towards Radical Innovations: The Case of the Self-Driving Car." p. 46.

Chapter 4: What Is the Future of Self-Driving Cars?

46. Iglinski and Babiak, "Analysis of the Potential of Autonomous Vehicles in Reducing the Emissions of Greenhouse Gases in Road Transport."

47. Quoted in Ricardo Daziano, "Are Consumers Willing to Pay to Let Cars Drive for Them? Analyzing Response to Autonomous Vehicles," *Elsevier Transportation Research Part C,* vol. 78, no. 150-164, 2017, p. 2.

48. Quoted in Daziano, "Are Consumers Willing to Pay to Let Cars Drive for Them? Analyzing Response to Autonomous Vehicles." p. 2.

49. Konig and Neumayr, "Users' Resistance Towards Radical Innovations: The Case of the Self-Driving Car." p. 48.

50. Quoted in Kang, "Self-Driving Cars' Prospects Rise With Vote by House."

51. Socker and Shaheen, "Shared Automated Vehicles: Review of Business Models."

52. Konig and Neumayr, "Users' Resistance Towards Radical Innovations: The Case of the Self-Driving Car."

53. California State Law, *Autonomous Vehicles,* http://leginfo.legislature.ca.gov.

54. Jack Boeglin, "The Costs of Self-Driving Cars: Reconciling Freedom and Privacy with Tort Liability in Autonomous Vehicle Regulation," *Yale Journal of Law and Technology*, vol. 17, no. 4, 2015, p. 15.

55. Carr, *The Glass Cage: Automation and Us*. p. 184.

56. Carr, *The Glass Cage: Automation and Us*. p. 186.

57. Quoted in Olivia Goldhill, "Philosophers are Building Ethical Algorithms to Help Control Self-Driving Cars," February 11, 2018. www.qz.com.

58. Carr, *The Glass Cage: Automation and Us*. p. 187.

59. Boeglin, "The Costs of Self-Driving Cars: Reconciling Freedom and Privacy with Tort Liability in Autonomous Vehicle Regulation." p. 32.

60. Kohl, "Disruption of Individual Mobility Ahead? A Longitudinal Study of Risk and benefit Perceptions of Self-Driving Cars of Twitter." p. 1224.

For Further Research

Books

Nicholas Carr, *The Glass Cage: Automation and Us*. New York: W. W. Norton & Company, Inc., 2014.

Kaitlen J. Exum and Lynn M. Messina, *The Car and Its Future*. New York: H. W. Wilson Company, 2004.

Lauren Newman, *Self-Driving Cars*. Ann Arbor, MI: Cherry Lake Publishing, 2018.

Gautam Shroff, *The Intelligent Web*. New York: Oxford University Press, 2013.

Sharon Weinberger, *The Imagineers of War*. New York: Alfred A. Knopf, 2017.

Internet Sources

Joel Barbier, "Self-Driving Cars Will Disrupt More Than the Auto Industry. Here Are the Winners and Losers," *CNBC*, May 3, 2017. www.cnbc.com.

Alex Davies, "An Oral History of the DARPA Grand Challenge, the Grueling Robot Race That Launched the Self-Driving Car," *Wired*, August 3, 2017. www.wired.com.

Eric Jaffe, "Why People Choose Cars, Even When Mass Transit Would Serve Them Better," *CityLab,* February 1, 2013. www.citylab.com.

Cecilia Kang, "Self-Driving Cars' Prospects Rise with Vote by House," *New York Times,* September 6, 2017. www.nytimes.com.

Jake Lingeman, "The 6 Levels of Autonomous Driving: Autoweek Explains," *Autoweek,* September 25, 2017. www.autoweek.com.

Aarian Marshall, "To Save the Most Lives, Deploy (Imperfect) Self-Driving Cars ASAP," *Wired*, November 7, 2017. www.wired.com.

Benjamin Preston, "Autonomy's Roadkill: The Path to Driverless Cars Will Be Strewn with the Carcasses of Big Industry," *Car and Driver*, February 26, 2016. blog.caranddriver.com.

Patrick Sisson, "As Self-Driving Cars Hit The Road, Real Estate Development May Take New Direction," *Curbed*, May 16, 2017. www.curbed.com.

Websites

Google's Self-Driving Car Project

www.google.com/selfdrivingcar

Internet and technology company Google has heavily invested in self-driving cars through its Waymo project.

National Highway Traffic Safety Administration

www.nhtsa.gov

The National Highway Traffic Safety Administration, part of the US Department of Transportation, supports safety in transportation. The agency is working to support development of self-driving cars that are safe.

Index

Index Continued

Image Credits

cover: © metamorworks/Shutterstock Images

4: © Linda Parton/Shutterstock Images

5: © Travis Wise CC2.0

8: © Sundry Photography/Shutterstock Images

12: © Tony Avelar/AP Images

15: © Zapp2Photo/Shutterstock Images

17: © Andrey_Popov/Shutterstock Images

20: © Red Line Editorial

24: © Travis Wise CC2.0

28: © egd/Shutterstock Images

31: © JasonDoiy/iStockphoto

35: © Gabrieletamborrelli/iStockphoto

42: © metamorworks/Shutterstock Images

44: © Sorbis/Shutterstock Images

47: © Scharfsinn/Shutterstock Images

49: © Eric Risberg/AP Images

50: © Yauhen_D/Shutterstock Images

52: © metamorworks/Shutterstock Images

55: © Sheila Fitzgerald/Shutterstock Images

58: © metamorworks/iStockphoto

61: © Bi Zhiyi/ImagineChina/AP Images

67: © Robert Crum/Shutterstock Images

68: © Sundry Photography/Shutterstock Images

About the Author

Jessica Mosloski is a writer, tea connoisseur, and corgi enthusiast based in Minneapolis, MN. She enjoys exploring unfamiliar places and driving around in her teal Mini Cooper, although she looks forward to the day when her Mini Cooper will be driving her around instead.